This edition published by Parragon in 2012
Parragon
Queen Street House
4 Queen Street
Bath BA1 1HE, UK
www.parragon.com

ISBN 978-1-4454-9281-0

Printed in China

5 Minute Bedtime Tale

Hansel
and
Gretel

Retold by Ronne Randall

Illustrated by Erica-Jane Waters

PaRRagon

Bath • New York • Singapore • Hong Kong • Cologne • Delhi
Melbourne • Amsterdam • Johannesburg • Auckland • Shenzhen

Hansel and Gretel lived by the forest with their stepmother and their father, who was a poor woodcutter.

One evening, the family had nothing to eat but a few crusts of bread. Hansel and Gretel went to bed feeling hungry. As they lay there, they heard their stepmother and father talking.

"There are too many mouths to feed," said their stepmother. "We must take your children into the forest and leave them there."

"Never!" cried their father.

"Well, I'm not going to starve," their stepmother shouted. "The children are going, and that is that!"

Gretel began to cry, but Hansel comforted her. "Don't worry. I'll think of something," he promised.

The next morning, Hansel and Gretel were woken by their stepmother at daybreak.

"We're going into the forest to chop wood," she cried, as she gave Hansel and Gretel a crust of bread each for their lunch.

Hansel broke his bread into tiny pieces.
As they walked along ...

... he secretly dropped a trail of crumbs on the ground.

"Your stepmother and I are going to chop wood now," the children's father said when they were deep in the forest. "We'll return for you at sunset."

The children shared Gretel's bread, and then they curled up at the foot of an old oak tree and fell asleep.

When Hansel and Gretel woke up, it was
dark and their little fire had gone out.

"Let's follow the trail of bread crumbs I left,"
whispered Hansel as he comforted his sister.

But the bread crumbs were gone!
The forest birds had eaten them all up.

"We'll wait until morning," Hansel said.
"When it's light, we'll find our way home."

TWIT-TWOO!

The next morning, the children
were woken by the sound of birdsong.
A white bird flapped its wings as if to
beckon them.

"Look!" cried Hansel. "Maybe that
bird will lead us home!"

But the white bird led them
deeper
into
the
forest
to a little house made of gingerbread!

The roof was dripping with frosting, the windows were framed with candy canes, and the garden was filled with lollipops.

Delighted, the hungry children began to feast upon the candies.

Suddenly, the door opened CR-R-REAK! and an old woman hobbled out.

"Nibble, nibble, like a mouse, who is nibbling at my house?"

she croaked. "I can't see very well—who are you?"

"Just two hungry children," Hansel replied.

"Ah," said the old woman, "well, you'd better come inside and I will make you a proper meal."

The old woman gave
Hansel and Gretel a plate
piled high with delicious
pancakes. They ate until
they were ready to burst!

Then she
showed them to
two little beds.
They snuggled
down under the
soft blankets and
fell fast asleep.

But Hansel and Gretel didn't know that the kind old woman was really a wicked witch.

"I'll soon fatten these two up," she cackled. "Then they will make a proper meal for ME!"

The following morning, the witch dragged Hansel from his bed and threw him into a cage.

"Give your brother a big breakfast," she ordered Gretel. "He is too skinny. I'll keep him locked up until he is nice and plump ...

... and then I'll EAT HIM UP!"

Every morning, over the next few days, the witch made
Hansel stick out his finger so she could feel whether he was
fat enough to eat.

But Hansel was clever. He knew the old witch
could hardly see, so he stuck a chicken bone through
the cage instead.

"Still too scrawny," the witch would say.

One day, the witch grew tired of waiting.

"Whether he be fatter or thinner,
I'll have Hansel for my dinner!"

she crowed.

"Light the oven!" the witch ordered Gretel. "Now crawl in and see whether it's hot enough."

Gretel knew the witch was planning to cook her as well, so she said, "The oven's much too small for me."

"Even I could fit inside that oven. Look!" said the witch, sticking her head inside.

This was Gretel's chance. She pushed the witch into the oven and slammed the door.

Gretel quickly freed Hansel from the cage.

"We're safe! Let's go home!" they sang happily.

There were chests full of gold and sparkling jewels in the witch's house. Hansel and Gretel filled their pockets before they left.

Back in the forest, the white bird was waiting to lead Hansel and Gretel home.

Their delighted father greeted them with hugs. He told them that their cruel stepmother had left. Hansel showed him the treasure they had found.

"We will never go hungry again!" he cried.

They all lived happily ever after.
And the white bird sat on their
rooftop and sang for them
every day.

The End